Canadian-born Shauna Taylor knew from a young age that she was a writer. After graduating from Nipissing University's English Literature program, she focused on writing in her spare time and growing a family of her own. While reading a bedtime story to her daughter and settling her fears of the darkened room, a story of courage and overcoming any fear, big or small, inspired her debut tale of *The Door.*

THE DOOR

SHAUNA TAYLOR

AUSTIN MACAULEY PUBLISHERS™
LONDON ∗ CAMBRIDGE ∗ NEW YORK ∗ SHARJAH

Copyright © Shauna Taylor (2021)

Ordering Information
Quantity sales: Special discounts are available on quantity purchases by corporations, associations, and others. For details, contact the publisher at the address below.

Publisher's Cataloging-in-Publication data
Taylor, Shauna
The Door

ISBN 9781649792648 (Paperback)
ISBN 9781649792655 (Hardback)
ISBN 9781649792679 (ePub e-book)
ISBN 9781649792662 (Audiobook)

Library of Congress Control Number: 2021902695

www.austinmacauley.com/us

First Published (2021)
Austin Macauley Publishers LLC
40 Wall Street, 33rd Floor, Suite 3302
New York, NY 10005
USA

mail-usa@austinmacauley.com
+1 (646) 5125767

To my three babies, Charlee, Fynlee and Kellan, you are and always will be my greatest adventure. Thank you for showing me that fear is nothing more than a door we must be brave enough to walk through.

To my incredible husband, Stefane, you have always been my biggest fan and my best friend. I owe this leap of faith to your unconditional love and support. Thank you always.

To my mother who always believed in me, even when I did not. Thank you for being the best mom always.

I lifted myself from the warmth of my four-post bed,
And walked feet slightly elevated to the large door
ahead. The door was closed and the knob was brass,
With twists and turns all in its clasp.
I reached for it, but not before,
I heard the laughter beyond the door.

I paused in wait for something more,

But all that stood was the silent door,

Quiet and still as it was before.

I reached again, my toes did strain,

I reached then jumped at the noise that came,

From a branch that tapped at my windowpane.

I tried my best to push back a sob,
And with one last stretch, I reached the knob.
Its brass was cold against my touch,
But open it I knew I must.
Though before I could, the knob did jiggle.
I jumped and scattered back to my bed;
Pulling the covers high above my head.
I laid there still as though asleep,
Listening as the door went creak.

She peaked inside, her curls came first,
Her dark black top with bright white pearls,
But all was still so the door she closed,
Which left a chill against my toes.

I lay a moment or maybe two,
The lump in my tummy once small now grew.
Though as moments past and silence followed,
I took in a breath and one quick swallow.
I lowered the sheets just a bit past my chin,
I could see though the darkness was full to the brim.

I laid in silence as the moments passed,
Watching a pale glow that the moon light cast.
I could feel my eyes, they were not like before;
They were heavier now as I stared at the door.
As the moments went on and the silence did follow,
My eyes grew heavier my mind grew more hollow.

I was almost asleep in the warmth of my bed,
When I heard a loud sound that made me sit
up instead.
Again the laugh rang, though not as faint as before,
The laughing that had come from beyond my large
bedroom door,
Seemed much closer now than it once had before.

For this laugh did not sound like the rest,
I listened through my heartbeat loud in my chest.
The laughing was not down the hall,
Or whispering through the creaks in the wall.

It was no longer beyond as it once was before.
This laughter it came from closer it seemed,
I did all I could and tried not to scream.

I shut my eyes and pulled the covers up close,
For I feared that it must be some kind of ghost.
But I am all by myself, I thought to myself,
Though laughing still rang through that old
darkened house.

I peeked out one eye and looked once more,
At the larger now darker old bedroom door.
It stood taller and darker than it had moments before,
Taller and darker against the cold bedroom floor.

I pulled down the covers and examined the floor,
For I noticed a light that had not been there before.
It was pink with some white, though the crack was
quite tight,
But I saw it shine through for it blinded my sight.

A shadow then passed, only one maybe two,
I placed my nails in my mouth and I started to chew.
The laughing was loud it did not stop like before,
It was loud, and I was sure now that it came from
the door,
Not from beyond like it once had before.

I looked at its tall and menacing gaze,
Suddenly the room before dark now covered in haze.
The light made my eyes squint so I rubbed them
a little,
And I saw my mom's face and started to giggle.
Her pearls and dark top, those blonde curls on
her head,
All looked at me with worry that I had not gone
to bed.

She lifted the blankets to no more than my chin,
And I looked towards the door where the laughing
had been.
Standing in silence it looked not like before,
It stood in its frame nothing more than a door.

She kissed me goodnight and she sang me a song,
For it turned out there was nothing to fear of the door
all along.

THE END

CPSIA information can be obtained
at www.ICGtesting.com
Printed in the USA
LVHW071048140521
687441LV00009B/130